Little Grey Rabbit's Valentine

The Little Grey Rabbit Library

Little Grey Rabbit's Valentine

Alison Uttley
pictures by Margaret Tempest

Collins

William Collins Sons & Co Ltd
London · Glasgow · Sydney · Auckland
Toronto · Johannesburg

First published 1953
© text The Alison Uttley Literary Property Trust 1988
© illustrations The Estate of Margaret Tempest 1988
© this arrangement William Collins Sons & Co Ltd 1988
Cover decoration by Fiona Owen
Decorated capital by Mary Cooper
Alison Uttley's original story has been abridged for this book.
Uttley, Alison
Little Grey Rabbit's Valentine. —
Rev. ed. — (Little Grey Rabbit books)
I. Title II. Tempest, Margaret
III. Series
823'.912 [J] PZ7

ISBN 0-00-194228-X

Typeset by Columns of Reading
Made and Printed in Great Britain by
William Collins Sons and Co Ltd, Glasgow

FOREWORD

Of course you must understand that Grey Rabbit's home had no electric light or gas, and even the candles were made from pith of rushes dipped in wax from the wild bees' nests, which Squirrel found. Water there was in plenty, but it did not come from a tap. It flowed from a spring outside, which rose up from the ground and went to a brook. Grey Rabbit cooked on a fire, but it was a wood fire, there was no coal in that part of the country. Tea did not come from India, but from a little herb known very well to country people, who once dried it and used it in their cottage homes. Bread was baked from wheat ears, ground fine, and Hare and Grey Rabbit gleaned in the cornfields to get the wheat.

The doormats were plaited rushes, like country-made mats, and cushions were stuffed with wool gathered from the hedges where sheep pushed through the thorns. As for the looking-glass, Grey Rabbit found the glass, dropped from a lady's handbag, and Mole made a frame for it. Usually the animals gazed at themselves in the still pools as so many country children have done. The country ways of Grey Rabbit were the country ways known to the author.

Robin the Postman stood in the shelter of the holly bush, staring down at a heap of letters. "It will take me hours to sort all these," he sighed. "St Valentine's Day tomorrow, and all these little messages to be delivered. I shall want help. I need an ass-ass-assistant. I can't do it. I really can't."

He turned over the tiny leafy envelopes with his beak, and flipped them with his wing and pushed them with his slender toes. Most of them were holly leaves but a few were brown beech leaves, and one was a cabbage leaf.

"Scores of Valentines, and who can be trusted to help? Not a bird can I ask, they will all be too busy billing-and-cooing, getting their love-songs ready, wetting their whistles. It's their courting day tomorrow."

Footsteps came padding along the lane, and Milkman Hedgehog came up with his milk cans. "Hello, Robin," said he, and he stopped and looked in astonishment.

"What's this? A windy day brought down all these, Robin?" he asked.

"Valentines," said Robin. "I'm snowed under with them."

"Why, it's St Valentine's Day tomorrow!" cried old Hedgehog. "I must send my missis one. Something short and sweet, like:

> 'Prickles is sharp and so are you
> You're still my sweetheart
> I love you true'."

The Robin wasn't listening.

"Milkman Hedgehog," said he suddenly. "Could you help me to deliver these Valentines tomorrow?" he asked.

"Me?" cried Hedgehog. "I can't read."

"No need. There are pictures on most of them," said Robin. "You can carry them in your milkcans. I'll sort them out and make it easy for you. Do help me," pleaded the Robin. "I'll lend you my second-best postman's hat, too. You'll be the assistant postman."

"Assistant postman? Well, well," hesitated the Hedgehog.

"Come here at dawn, when you've done milking, and I'll give you the Valentines," said the Robin.

"And the hat," added Hedgehog. "They won't believe it unless I wear a hat."

"Yes, the hat," cried the Robin cheerfully and he began to whistle and sing.

Old Hedgehog went on his way to the cows, and then he turned home.

"I'm going to help Postman Robin tomorrow, wife," said he. "It's St Valentine's Day and he's extra busy. I'm going to wear a postman's hat," added the Hedgehog. "It makes me official, like."

Mrs Hedgehog was delighted and Fuzzypeg danced with joy.

"My father's going to be a postman," he boasted up and down the lanes and fields.

"Whatever for?" asked Water Rat who was polishing his boat.

"It's St Valentine's Day tomorrow," said Fuzzypeg.

Water Rat counted the notches on a post by the river; one, two, three, up to thirteen. "February the Fourteenth tomorrow. St Valentine's Day," said he. "I must post my Valentine tonight."

The little Hedgehog danced away to Grey Rabbit's house and tapped on the door.

"Come in Fuzzypeg," Grey Rabbit cried. "I've been baking blackberry jam puffs, and here's one for you, hot from the oven."

"My father's going to be a postman tomorrow," said Fuzzypeg, as he took a big bite of the jam puff.

"Surely not!" cried Grey Rabbit.

"Yes, he's going to be a postman and wear a hat because Postman Robin wants a sister to help him, for St Valentine's."

"A sister for St Valentine's," shouted Hare and he leapt high.

"St Valentine's," echoed Squirrel, spinning round so rapidly her tail flew out in the wind.

"I must be going," said Fuzzypeg. "Thank you, dear Grey Rabbit."

"Goodbye, Fuzzypeg," they all called, and away he went to spread his news.

"What is a Valentine, Grey Rabbit?" asked Squirrel.

"It's a picture or a message for one you love, and you mustn't put your name. It's a surprise," said Grey Rabbit.

"Then how do you know who sent it?" asked Hare.

"You try to guess," said Grey Rabbit.

"Well, I'm going to make my Valentine now," said Hare. "And me too," said Squirrel, and Grey Rabbit nodded.

They all sat down at the table with pen and ink and paint-brushes and leaves. The pens were quills from the goose, and the brushes were made of feathers which the Speckledy Hen gave them. The ink was the juice of a flower, and the paints were made of flower petals.

A great scratching came from Hare's pen and he stuck out his tongue as he wrote.

"Who's going to have your Valentine, Hare?" whispered Squirrel very softly so that Grey Rabbit would not hear.

"It's for the Fox," whispered Hare. "I'm doing a special Valentine for him."

"But he's not your special friend," protested Squirrel.

"I'm sending it to my special enemy," said Hare.

Squirrel stared. She licked her quill pen and waited. "How do you spell Love, Grey Rabbit?" she asked loudly.

"L-O-V-E," said Grey Rabbit.

"I thought that was for a loaf of bread," said Squirrel.

"I'm good at rhyming," boasted Hare.
"Love, Dove."

He dipped his pen in the ink and he began to write. "Fox, Box, Nox, Wox," he muttered, and he made his Valentine.

"Mister Fox.
You'll get some Nox.
Beware.
From Hare."

He lighted a candle and sealed his letter with scarlet sealing-wax so that it looked like a holly berry on the holly leaf.

"You are clever, Hare," said Squirrel, enviously. "I can't do mine."

"Put your thinking-cap on," said Hare, and Squirrel tied her handkerchief in a bonnet on her head.

"It has worked," she cried. "The thinking-cap helped me. I can do it now."

She scribbled for a few minutes and then read aloud her Valentine:

> "'When this you see
> Remember me,
> And drink your tea.'

"It is for Moldy Warp," she explained.

Grey Rabbit was struggling with her Valentine, which was for Wise Owl because nobody else would send him one.

"Lend me your thinking-cap, Squirrel," said she. "I can't do it."

She went to her writing-desk, and at once she
wrote Wise Owl's message:

> "The Owl is wise,
> He's full of eyes,
> And when he cries
> Too-whit, too-whoo,
> I love him too,
> I do, I do."

She had to take three holly leaves and pin
them together to make her long Valentine for
the Owl.

"I'll give them to the Robin," said Hare.

While the three animals were busy making
their Valentines, Water Rat leapt in his boat
and rowed out to the middle of the stream.
There, with ducks laughing at him, he wrote
on a lily-leaf, then threw it away, for all he
could say was "Love, Dove."

He rowed back to the shore and hurried to his home.

"Oh, Mrs Webster, do help me to make a Valentine," he cried to his housekeeper. "It won't rhyme."

"I know nothing of rhymes," said fat Mrs Webster, "but I can make some nice Valentines, such as any young person would like to get. Just leave it to me."

Mrs Webster went back to the kitchen, where she made some St Valentine's cakes, of duck eggs and sugar and butter. She looked in her cupboard for the St Valentine's cutter, which was in the shape of a heart. She cut a dozen little yellow cakes, and dropped a dried camomile flower on each. Then she baked them in the oven, and left them to cool.

On St Valentine's Day the birds were singing very early to one another, for every bird got up at dawn to sing to his dearest one.

"What a noise the birds are making," yawned Hare.

"It's St Valentine's Day," Grey Rabbit reminded him. "It's the birds' courting day and they sing to their sweethearts."

"Hum," grunted Hare. "Sweethearts. I could do with a sweet heart for breakfast. I'm hungry. I'd like a heart made of sugar and spice."

"There's a dove calling. Listen," said Squirrel.

"Coo-roo. Coo-roo. I love true." cooed the dove in the tree. Hare went to the door and looked out.

Old Hedgehog was already coming with the milk. He carried one pail of milk and one pail of letters. On his head a tiny black hat was perched.

"Good morning, everybody," said he. "I'm the assistant postman. A happy St Valentine's Day to you. Here's a Valentine for Miss Grey Rabbit, and one for Miss Squirrel and two for Mister Hare."

"Oh, thank you. Thank you, kind assistant postman," said the three, and they carried their Valentines to the table. Milkman Hedgehog filled the jug with new milk and stood for a moment on the doorstep.

"I've been very busy," he informed them.
"I've got Valentines for all the rabbits, hares,
hedgehogs, field mice and whatnot in the
district. I don't know what's come over the
animals this year. There wasn't all this
Valentining when I was young. Only the
birds sent Valentines, but now everybody's
doing it."

"It's a nice custom," said Grey Rabbit.

"That reminds me, I've got another
Valentine for you, Miss Grey Rabbit. I put it
in my pocket for safety, and I nearly forgot
it."

He pulled out a snow-white square
envelope, addressed to Little Grey Rabbit. In
the corner was a stamp, nearly as big as the
letter.

"Who can have sent this?" asked Grey Rabbit, turning it over and examining it carefully. It was sealed with green wax.

"Open it and see," cried Hare, impatiently.

"Yes, open it," added Squirrel, dancing with excitement.

Slowly Grey Rabbit broke the seal and opened the white envelope. She drew out a picture of a heart, painted with tiny flowers round the edge, and "Dear Grey Rabbit" printed on it.

"Who sent it?" she asked, but Hedgehog didn't know. Robin had given it to him with the rest and he had asked no questions.

"I mustn't waste time. I've these Valentines to deliver as well as my milk. Good morning, Miss," said he.

"Good morning, Hedgehog," said Grey Rabbit. Then she ran after him and pressed a tiny bottle of violet scent into his hand.

"For you, dear Milkman," she whispered.

Squirrel and Hare were reading their leafy letters. Squirrel had a nut tied to hers, and a few words were pricked on the leaf.

> "Sweet Lavender, Sweet Lavender.
> A Valentine lies under her."

Squirrel darted out to the garden, and there under the lavender bush lay a leafy parcel with a white wool muff, lined with scarlet.

"I do believe my Valentine is from you, Grey Rabbit," cried Squirrel. "Nobody else knew how much I wanted a white muff for these cold February days. Thank you, dear Grey Rabbit."

Hare opened his letter and read aloud the message written in large clumsy letters on a cabbage leaf.

> "O Hare so sweet,
> Will you be mine?
> I bid you meet
> Your Valentine."

"Oh! Oh!" cried Hare leaping high so that his coat tails went out like wings. "Did you hear that?"

"'O Hare so sweet'," said Squirrel, mocking. "Are you sweet?"

"'Will you be mine?'" said Grey Rabbit slowly. "Who wants you to be theirs? Who wants to meet you, Hare?"

Hare stopped and sniffed his Valentine. They all wrinkled their noses and sniffed.

"It's not violets. I gave that to Old Hedgehog," said Grey Rabbit.

"It's not lily-of-the-valley," said Squirrel. "I put a drop of that on Mole's Valentine."

"It's – it's – it's Fox!" shuddered Hare. "I remember it. He sent me this Valentine."

"Never mind, Hare. Here's a second Valentine the postman brought you."

Grey Rabbit pointed to a green leaf which had fallen to the floor.

"Darling Hare,
The Hare we love,
Look on the chair,
Below and above."

Hare ran to the rocking-chair. On the seat
lay a little parcel and under the chair was
another. He opened them and drew out first a
cobweb waistcoat with a heart embroidered
on it, and then a scarlet handkerchief for his
pocket.

"This is from you, Grey Rabbit,"
he cried. "I know it. Oh, thank you.
It's just what I want.
What a lovely Valentine."

There was a rat-tat-tat on the door. Water Rat stood there with Mrs Webster. They carried an elegant basket made of reeds from the river.

"A basket of Valentines for Miss Grey Rabbit," said Mrs Webster, curtseying. Water Rat bowed and shook his frills.

"Come in. Come in," invited Grey Rabbit.

They entered and although they brought pools of water from their clothes, nobody minded. Grey Rabbit opened the basket and saw the dozen little golden cakes in the shape of hearts.

"I was so hungry," said Hare.

"This is a sensible Valentine. Thank you Water Rat and Mrs Webster."

Mrs Webster was peeping about, for she had never seen the little house before. Grey Rabbit popped a jar of heather honey in her pocket and gave Water Rat a lace frill for his coat.

Wise Owl's present fell down the chimney. It was a little book called "The True History of the Valentine," but it had so many hard words Hare used it as a footstool.

Fuzzypeg came with his Valentine. It was a basket of snowdrops from the woods. Speckledly Hen of course sent an egg but it had the word LUV scrawled on it by the Hen's big toe.

"Who sent your special Valentine?" asked everybody as they looked at the white envelope with a real stamp and a flowery heart.

"Who sent it, Grey Rabbit?"

Grey Rabbit shook her head. She had no idea.

"I think it was Moldy Warp," said Squirrel, but when the Mole came, he said "No." He brought a tiny silver locket which he had made out of a sixpence he once found. It was the prettiest little locket and it opened to hold a drop of dew.

They all stood in a circle and sang the Valentine song, in thanks for all the presents and love.

"St Valentine's Day. St Valentine's Day. The birds are courting and kissing today. We love one another whatever you say. We are very happy this Valentine's Day."

But who sent the Valentine? Perhaps it was a Fairy, or even St Valentine himself. I cannot tell you for it is my secret, but perhaps it was a little boy or girl. I leave you to guess.

DEAR
GREY
RABBIT